THE NEW WIFE

THE NEVER AFTERS

THE NEW WIFE

A NEVER AFTERS TALE

KIRSTYN M^CDERMOTT

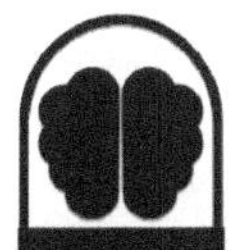

Brain Jar Press
PO Box 6687
Upper Mt Gravatt, QLD, 4122
Australia
www.BrainJarPress.com

Cover design by Peter Ball
Cover Image: *Old Key*, Arctic Ice/Shutterstock; *Blood Stains*, Bogdan Ionscue/Shutterstock

ISBN: 978-1-922479-32-7 (Ebook) | 978-1-922479-31-0 (Chapbook)

THE NEW WIFE

The chamber floor is clotted with blood, and my fine silk slippers skid on the tiles, soaking themselves scarlet. Dove grey, they were, shot through with brightest blue: the colour of the vast and changeable oceans they travelled to reach my soft little feet; the colour of my absent husband's beard. Faint, I hold on to the marble basin that stands in the centre of the room and try not to consider its gruesome contents.

Will I ever be rid of what I've seen in this place? Will—

I need to leave.

I need to fetch my brothers from the inn where I pray they're still staying, and rouse the town guard as well. Bring them all, muskets and sabres and neat black moustaches, bring them to this wretched basement so they may see for themselves what breed of monster it is I have married.

My brothers will know what to do; they will keep me safe from his wrath.

The door is shut, though I don't remember closing it; the handle turns but doesn't yield. I press my ear to the dark wood, expecting—what? The sound of breathing from the other side? A rumble of laughter, low and limned with cruelty, or the eager, ominous shuffle of boots on stone? All these things, and none of them, and it's none of them I hear. My heart settles its fearful pace. The door had swung shut behind me, that's all. Swung shut and locked itself, as some doors are made to do, with my mind too consumed by horrors to pay heed.

But where's the key? Not in my hands or the pockets of my skirts, though I pat frantically through the voluminous folds, turning about to retrace my steps until I spy the thing, bright and golden, all but floating in the middle of a gleaming, viscous pool.

The blood wipes off easily enough. The brass polishes clean.

Until, lifting key to lock — oh, me! — that dauntless red seeps back again. And again, and again; no matter how vigorous my attempts to vanquish the stain, it will not budge for more than the span of a desperate, long-held breath.

"There'll be no hiding that, my dear. Not from him."

The woman drifts loose of the shadows, her pale throat bearing a gash so deep I can see the flash of bone through the pulse and twitch of severed flesh. Blood drips from the wound as she moves; the bodice of her lilac gown shines as dark as the skin of bruised plums. She bears some resemblance to the corpse on the far wall, the one whose yellow hair is matted dull with cobwebs.

"You'll not be rid of it," the woman says, "no matter how much rubbing you do."

Her voice isn't the voice of any living soul. I can feel it in my teeth.

"Who are *you* to speak so boldly to me?" I draw myself upright, hitch my shoulders straight and pray my trembling falls beneath her notice. "Here, in my own home, uninvited and ... and ... shabby as a beggar-maid."

The woman laughs, throat agape. Then—

—she is standing right before me, narrow face scarce inches from my own. I cry out and stumble backwards till my spine is pressed against the door.

"Your home?" the woman sneers. "*I* married the man to whom this house belongs. *I* dressed the dining room windows with drapes of fine damask, and brought as dowry the silverware with which you eat your supper. This is *my* home, little girl, and I shall speak as bold as I please within its walls."

"We all married him, Charlotte." A second figure comes into

view. She wears a mint-green dress and holds both hands to her stomach; blood oozes through the splay of her fingers. "We're all his wives, with this one no different for breathing."

The first woman, the woman called Charlotte, snorts. "That's all the difference in the world, Gabrielle." Grey eyes glitter within dark and hollow sockets. I think of the brooch my mother gave me the night before my wedding, delicate marquisette passed down from *her* mother, and *her* mother before that, the only item of value I could bring to the marriage — apart from the throb of maidenhood between my thighs, a bauble my husband swiftly claimed.

"A petty distinction," Gabrielle says, "with so little time for it to matter."

My jaw clenches as I notice the shapes of two other women behind her, with a third hovering at their heels. "How—how many of you are there?"

Charlotte turns to follow my gaze. "This is the whole of us. Five wives, soon to be six."

"Seven." The voice is soft and tremulous.

"Six," Charlotte repeats firmly.

A short, slim figure glides forth. Her hair is a limp and sodden mass of brunette curls, and I can only guess at how pretty her face must have been before someone stove in the left side of her skull. My husband adores a pretty face above all else; he's told me so on several occasions. The slim woman shakes her head; her left eye bulges and rolls in a strange and sickening fashion. "Seven," she insists.

Instantly, the two remaining women are by her side. "Hush, Marie-Catherine," says the one wrapped in a jonquil robe, the one whose neck is ringed by a livid scorch of rope. She wraps an arm around Marie-Catherine's shoulders. The other woman, tall with broad, gentle hips swathed in blushing pink, bends to whisper into Marie-Catherine's ear. She folds her arms like wings behind her back and my eyes are drawn to her wrists, their stumps raw and red and dripping.

Bile rises in my throat and I swallow, sagging against the door as my vision wavers and fogs.

"What an innocent we have found," Charlotte says. "A babe in the woods!"

The woman in pink turns her head to regard me with a mild, incurious gaze. Then she opens her mouth, wide and wet and dark, and coughs a bloody chunk of gore onto the tiles at her feet. There is no time to look away, no time to dodge the knowing of it.

"Marie-Jeanne, really." Quick as blinking, the woman in the jonquil robe scoops the tongue up from the floor, holds it to her companion's mouth the way a groom might offer an apple to a horse, fingers stretched flat and steady. Marie-Jeanne accepts it, sucks the severed piece of flesh through thin, pale lips and smiles. Blood smears her chin. The woman in the jonquil robe cleans it away with a lace-edged handkerchief tugged from her sleeve.

"Enough parlour games," Charlotte snaps.

Marie-Jeanne grins at me, her teeth red.

"Poor little dove," says the woman in the jonquil robe.

Charlotte rolls her eyes. "That's sympathy gone to waste, Henriette. The snivelling wretch brought it on herself, same as we all did."

It's enough to goad my voice from hiding. "Was it me who did all this?" I wave at the bodies hung about the chamber walls, those deathly still relics of the women gathered before me. "Was it my hand that slit your throat?"

"'Twas your hand that opened the door, *little dove*. 'Tis your hand that holds the key this very moment."

I glance down, finding the stain even brighter now against the brass, glossy and gleaming and fresh. "Help me." The words crack on my tongue, and I swallow hard as I hold the key out, this soiled and paltry offering. "Help me clean it."

"It will never come clean," Charlotte says. "Not till your own blood is spilled."

The woman in the jonquil robe, the woman called Henriette, smiles at me. "As ours has been spilled. As we deserved." Her voice is kind, and so are her eyes. "Do not fret; it will likely be swift."

Beside her, Marie-Jeanne shakes her head and extends her stumps.

Henriette squeezes the woman's shoulder. "He does not take the time these days, dearheart. He is quick about it." She looks at Charlotte, whose bone-white fingers are now at her own wounded throat, fiddling with a clean-cut edge. "Too quick."

"But I've done nothing wrong," I say.

Gabrielle steps forward, bloody hands still clutching her midsection as though holding herself together, as though holding herself within. "You've seen him for what he is."

"You broke your promise," Henriette says.

"You disobeyed." Charlotte leans in close to me, nose wrinkling. "No one to blame but yourself. He asked one thing of you, forbade you but one room in this whole great house, and yet here you stand before us, a scarce two days since he left."

"I withstood temptation a whole fortnight," Henriette informs me.

"I had the key in the lock while the wheels of his coach still rattled down the drive," Gabrielle says.

Charlotte favours her with a withering glare. "Yes, yes. We are all aware of your unmitigated haste."

The key is warm in my hand, slick and dagger-sly, and I thrust it in Charlotte's direction. "But he *gave* us the key — he wanted us to come in here, can't you see? It was a trap."

"It was a test," Charlotte says. "And none of us worthy of his faith. Six wives, and not a one as loyal as even the most dejected cur."

"Seven," whispers Marie-Catherine.

"Henriette, can you not have that mad creature keep her peace?"

"Hush now, dearheart." Henriette pats Marie-Catherine's cheek and rearranges the woman's curls to better fill the sickening hollow in the side of her head. "It will be over again soon."

Seven. This time the number catches, an insistent child tugging on the ragged hem of my thoughts, and I push past the women, push *through* the women, their forms offering less impediment than morning fog on a carriageway. My index finger shakes as I count the corpses in the room, count them and match what remains of their garments to the gowns worn by their spectral counterparts.

Seven.

"Who is she?" I point to a small, crumpled pile of dark blue fabric in the corner. How many years before she rotted down to bones?

"No one that need concern you," Charlotte says.

"She isn't here. Why isn't she here?"

Marie-Catherine lifts her head in my direction. Her right eye holds my gaze; the left rolls dangerously in its misshapen socket. "First."

"Need I tear out your damnable tongue myself?" Charlotte turns on the woman with hands outstretched, fingers curled to fearsome claws, but Henriette steps neatly between them. The expression on her face could shatter steel.

I stare at Marie-Catherine. "First ... wife?"

The barest glimmer of a smile lifts the corner of her mouth.

"First wife," I repeat, speaking to Charlotte now, and to the rest of them. "And what did *she* do then, to deserve such a fate? What could she possibly have seen that he needed to silence her for it?"

Charlotte glowers. "Perhaps that is why she is not here." She flicks a seething glance towards Marie-Catherine, who shrinks down into her own hunched shoulders. "Perhaps that is why *we do not speak of her.*"

Gabrielle glides forward and takes Charlotte by the hand. "Save your words," she tells me. "There will be more time for talking amongst ourselves later. More time and less confusion, you shall see."

"Run along, lovely," Henriette urges. "He won't be long now."

Expectation sharpens their features as they herd me towards the chamber door. Charlotte, Gabrielle, Henriette and even poor Marie-Jeanne, mouth pressed to a red-lipped smirk, all of them ushering me on my way. *Count the hours left to you, lovely. He will be coming, little dove. Listen for the rattle of coach wheel on cobbles.*

Await the clatter of iron-shod hooves. Only Marie-Catherine lingers behind, watchful face half-hidden by blood-draggled curls, slim hands wringing themselves into knots.

My younger brother, Charles, does the same thing when he's anxious.

My brothers. Oh, my brothers, *my brothers.*

I could weep with the relief of it. "I don't need your help," I tell the wives, unlocking the door and pulling it open. "My brothers are in town awaiting orders from their garrison. Once I fetch them, they'll see to it my husband is hanged for these vile crimes. Hanged, or worse."

Charlotte cocks her head. "Brothers, is it? Off you go then, little dove."

"You—you can all stay here and rot." I lock the door behind me and shove the key deep into my skirt pocket. Though the wives do not follow, their laughter pursues me all the way down the corridor, crowding my head with scorn and bitter glee.

I cannot leave the house.

It matters not which manner of egress I try — the heavy oak of the entrance door, the delicate glass that would on any other day usher me into the gardens, even this rude kitchen door by which my servant-girl Suzette comes and goes — the result is the same. As soon as I attempt to pass, my vision blurs and darkens, all breath is sucked from my lungs, and I find myself propelled backward, buffeted by an unseen storm within that roils and gusts and threatens to tear me asunder.

Palm pressed to my chest, I slump onto the slate tiles and wait for my heart to slow.

This house is a trap — a trap for wives, I fear, sprung by the same murderous sorcery that governs the key. My husband must surely be the Devil, or else has made the most vile of pacts with him. Tears prick afresh, but I don't bother to wipe them away. "Oh, my brothers," I whisper, "if only you could know your wretched sister's plight. If only you could hear her prayers."

In the hearth on the other side of the kitchen, a fire burns low beneath the soup-pot that Suzette has left to simmer. Thick, meaty aromas fill the air, and my stomach churns.

Run along, lovely. He won't be long now.

On the morning after my wedding night, I came downstairs to find my husband crouched by the fireplace in the parlour room, feeding the garments that I had so carefully packed and brought with me into the flames. My objections he silenced with a smile, and with a thumb pressed firm against my lips. *What need do you have of such rags, oh my beloved, when I can clothe you in finery beyond your dreams?* He kept me by his side, one arm encircling my waist, while he burned the remainder of my things. The fire raged so high and so hot I half-feared it would burst its confines and latch onto the hem of my robe, but my husband leaned ever closer, his face flushed and gleaming.

By the time he was done, nothing remained but ash.

Taking a deep breath, I push myself to my feet. Though I may not be able to escape this house, I can light a fire.

The flames consume the slippers with ardour, the slippers and my gown as well, its hem dragged red with trespass. But the stain on the key holds fast, glows with even greater vibrancy amid the lick and crackle of the flames, and my hands shake as they reach for yet more wood. If only I'd not sent Suzette to the village so laden with errands, if only I'd not been so eager to have the mansion — with *all* its rooms — entirely to myself. The girl might be sullen and not very bright, but she can stoke a fire with heat enough to bead the coldest brow.

Heat enough, surely, to burn blood from brass.

Failing that, she might know a scullery trick to do with salt or soured milk or such, some cunning ploy to clean the key as easily as she did my bridal linens, and—oh!

The front door opens with a sly creak then snicks closed again as my husband's voice booms down the entrance hall. "Beloved, I am home." Not due! Not due for many a day but still, these are his words, and these his boots, treading with ominous deliberation upon the floorboards. "Beloved, oh my beloved, where are you hiding yourself?"

Within the embers, the key gleams smug and sure.

There'll be no hiding that, child. Not from him.

I thrust the poker into a log burned near to crumbling and it groans apart, smothers my would-be telltale beneath cinders and ash. A hasty burial but needs must do; I'm not some mewling kitten, to be damned for curiosity. Forcing my mouth into a smile, lips catching dry over teeth, I turn to face my husband as he strides through the parlour door. It's not possible for him to have grown taller, for those shoulders to have broadened and bulked, and yet here he stands, looming over me in the manner of a bear roused from slumber, its once drowsy eyes now keen with appetite.

My hands tighten around the poker.

"Beloved," he says. "You have lost all your pretty colour!"

"You startled me. I had not expected you back so soon."

He reaches out and brushes the backs of his fingers over my cheek; it takes all of my will not to flinch. A messenger met him on horseback, he explains, with word that those matters of business which were to draw him abroad have been fortuitously resolved, and so of course he hastened back to be with his bride. Am I not happy to see him, he wants to know, plump lips pouting through the blue of his beard. Am I not elated to have my husband home again?

"But, of course," I assure him. "I only regret having been caught so unprepared." I smooth my hair and swish the hem of the dressing robe I'd donned before consigning my stained garments to the flames. Fortuitous news, fortuitous timing — or yet more of my husband's devilry.

He holds out his hand. "I'll have my keys."

I take the heavy, jangling ring from my pocket and place it in his palm.

"And the other one, oh my beloved?"

"Oh, that — that's tucked away safe upstairs in my rooms." I flutter my lashes as I've seen my mother do when trying to shave some coins from the price of a mutton leg. "Why would I have need to carry a thing I am forbidden to use?"

His smile stretches, as thin as the blade on a paring knife. "Fetch it for me."

I don't realise that I've glanced towards the fireplace until it's too late. Only for a moment, for less than a moment, but more than enough to catch his notice and he's upon me in two quick paces, one blunt-nailed hand seizing my wrist, the other wresting the poker from my grasp as he drags me over to the hearth. Ignoring my pleas and protestations, he pushes aside the burning logs and lumps of coal, scattering ash in a fine grey cloud, until, oh, there it lies — the wretched key, glistening with blood so bright it might have been fresh-spilled.

"Villainy!" My husband's eyes blaze as dark as brimstone. "Villainy and lies!"

I plead for him to let me loose, beggarly words that trip and thicken on my tongue. The door was barely opened, I assure him, and barely a single step did I take across the threshold, so dark was the forbidden room and cold as well, and so I saw nothing, if there even was a thing to see and this not some cruel trick that husbands play on new wives to test their love.

"Their obedience," he corrects me. "To test their obedience."

I lower my gaze. "I've been obedient in all else. As I shall continue to be, if only you can forgive me this one small transgression." He makes no reply at first and still I stand with head neatly bowed, trying not to consider the nakedness of my scalp, the fragility of bone beneath.

"Fetch my key," he says at last, releasing his hold on my wrist. His voice is softer now, edged with an anticipation that I recognise from our wedding night, but when I reach for the poker, my husband shakes his head and swings the tool beyond my reach. He nods at my hand, at my fingers bare and trembling. "Fetch it, beloved."

"It will burn me."

"Not if you are innocent as you claim. Have you not heard of such trials?"

"Those are for witches!"

"And adulteresses, and heretics, and liars of all stripes." He nods towards the fireplace and slaps the poker against the flat of his palm. "But if you are a Godly woman…"

Without allowing myself time to think, I crouch and scoop the key from the ashes, intending to cast the thing immediately at his feet, but my husband moves with viper speed, snatching my fist in his own and squeezing so tight I cannot tell which hurts more, the crush of bone against bone, or the sear of brass into flesh.

For an eternity, such agony is the entire sum of my being.

When I can no longer scream, when the only sound that can claw its way from my throat is a cracked and broken whimper, he tosses me aside, allowing me to crumple to the floor with my poor hand curled to my breast. The key falls at last from my grasp, still bloody and bright, awaiting the death that shall cleanse it.

"You are all alike," my husband mutters. "Wicked, wicked women." He raises the poker above his head. Such a sharp point it has, and so savage that little spike that juts out near its tip like the fighting spur on a rooster. Strange, how I've never had cause before to notice. So strange.

Close your eyes, little dove.

And I do.

But the expected blow does not land. Instead, there comes the thump of booted feet and urgent, shouted voices, and I lift my head to see — oh! my answered prayers! — my brothers storming into the parlour with sabres drawn and gleaming.

"What is the meaning of this?" Pierre demands of my husband. Charles moves to approach me, but our older brother stays him with an outstretched arm.

"Your sister lacks obedience," my husband says. "She requires instruction, which you cannot deny is both my right and my duty to administer. In truth, young sirs, you furnished me a spoiled, irresponsible child — am I expected to leave her untempered?"

The moment swells, thickens with indecision. Even Charles seems to hesitate, and I cannot bear it, cannot bear the thought of them, my own brothers, deferring and retreating and leaving me to the mercy of this monster. I lift my hand, brandishing the bleeding, seeping wound like a witch's mark. "He killed them," I croak. "His other wives, he killed them all."

With a roar, my husband sinks his boot deep into my stomach. I gasp, my throat closing on breathless space. I cannot move, can do no more than curl on the rug, eyes fixed on the newly raised poker—

Close your eyes, little dove.

—and then my brothers are upon him.

Steel flashes, slicing through flesh. Again, and again, until that massive frame falters and finally falls to the floor beside me. He gapes, my husband, mouth opening and closing like a trout on the block, his life pooling thick and red and hot, spilling and spreading across the fine Turkish weave upon which we both lie. His eyes, I notice for the first time, are as blue as his beard. And how they burn, even now, even with his last breath, how they burn!

At night, the halls of this great house are as dark and cold as the tombs of kings, and the flame from my candle provides little warmth. The front door looms before me, its whorled carvings of leaf and flower seeming to shiver in the flickering light as I place the candlestick on the floor, nudging it to one side with my toe. My injured right hand is useless, bound in swathes of linen that Suzette changes three times a day. The wound will not stop bleeding, though the army surgeon whom Charles fetched dismissed it as a trivial thing, so concerned was he about my nerves.

I have been confined to bed now for five days, during which time my brothers have kept themselves busy, dealing with the constabulary and other long-nosed men of law, spurning the ever inquisitive villagers, those men and women and tribes of eager-eyed children all salivating for a glimpse of the slaughterhouse.

Charles tells me nothing, of course, but Suzette has no such qualms.

Witchcraft, Madame, that's all the talk at market. Witchcraft and sorcery and how his lordship must've made some high bargain with the Devil, getting away with it as long as he did, or maybe how he was the Devil, and maybe — those muddy brown eyes flicking up to meet my own, as sly as pennies for the dead — *maybe how you've had dealings yourself, being as how you're the only one left alive of all them poor ladies, and not once shown your face since they brung out all them bodies. Not that I believe such talk, Madame, not I that knows you.*

Her words chill me. Who can guess what gossip the girl takes with her to market, what flames she likely fans for the sake of new-found infamy? I wish her gone and have said as much to Charles, but he insists there is no one else in the village who will come work here. Still, I do not trust Suzette and the close, appraising manner with which she looks at every scrap of chattel in this house. She looks at me most keenly of all.

The brass handle is cool beneath my touch. It turns easily, the door swinging inward with the barest sigh. Outside, the moonless sky is dark and the world is silent and unstirring.

Though I take slow and careful steps, the instant my foot touches the threshold it comes, just as it did before, a tremendous pressure as painful as stays pulled past bearing. I slam the door, then press my back against it, dragging air into my lungs. I had hoped that my husband's sorcery would have dissipated with his death. My brothers have been able to come and go at will these past few days, and so has Suzette. But as for myself—

"We cannot leave," a voice whispers from the dark. The woman with the stoved-in face — Marie-Catherine? Marie-Jeanne? — is right beside me. She sees me staring, ducks her head and reaches up to pull more of those sodden brunette curls over the injured side. Embarrassed, I shift my gaze to the dress she wears, those billows of pale peach silk with tiny pink roses stitched around the hem. Such fine work would have come at no small expense.

"You're still here," I say. "I had thought, with your bodies laid to rest..."

My brothers took care of such matters with all due haste. They contacted the families of my husband's former wives, what families could be found, and saw to it that their lost daughters, their lost sisters, were returned to them. Only the bones in the blue dress, the oldest bones, the bones of the first wife, remained unidentified. They could find no record of her among my husband's papers and no one in the village owned to ever being aware of her existence. She is buried, her grave marked but bearing no name, in the churchyard. At my insistence, the vicar's purse was weighted with enough coin to ensure a proper Christian burial. It was the least, the very least, our husband's money could do.

"We cannot leave," the woman says again. "We wore the ring. We used the key."

"But he's dead now." Dead and burned to greasy ash on a pyre with all the village circled around, spitting and singing hymns to the sky. Suzette told me that, her tone deadpan yet somehow conveying an unsavoury glee. "Shouldn't his spells die with him?"

She shakes her head. "Not spells. Worse than spells. Colder."

"Marie-Catherine, here you are!" The woman in the jonquil robe, the one with the hideous rope burn around her neck, drifts towards us from the other end of the hall. "Come, dearheart, leave this lady in peace." She puts an arm around Marie-Catherine's shoulders and touches her cheek with a gentle hand.

"Henriette?"

She looks at me with one eyebrow arched.

"That is your name? Henriette?"

"It is."

"Can you help me? I want—I need to leave this place."

"Wants and needs hold no water. You made your bed, same as the rest of us."

"But I'm not like you. I'm not dead." The expression on her face is so piteous, so motherly, even though she could not have been more than a year or two my elder when last she drew a living breath, that I falter, finding no words save the echo of those already spoken which, less assured now, splinter on my tongue. "I am *not* dead."

"No," Henriette says, her voice kind. "Not yet."

At her side, Marie-Catherine shivers and laces thin fingers together as though in prayer. Prayer, or supplication. "Not safe."

"Yes, dearheart, I know." Henriette raises a finger to her lips, stares straight at me and—

—vanishes. The two of them, simply gone.

A damp and bone-numbing chill seeps in to the hall, bringing with it a blackness so dense it crushes the light of my candle to a pinprick and a silence that robs all sound from the world save the unmistakable hiss of a single indrawn breath.

"Beloved," my husband whispers into my ear. "Where is my key?"

Hysteria, the surgeon deems it, with my brothers in whole-hearted agreement. What else could have compelled me to wander barefoot through the house in the middle of the night? What else could explain the bloodcurdling screams that dragged them from their beds and led them to find me huddled in the entrance hall, fingers knotted in my hair and babbling all manner of nonsense about ghosts and graves and husbands back from the dead? Hysteria accounts too for the seeping wound on my hand, the brand still as fresh as the moment my husband made it — *why, the poor girl's body cannot even heal itself when her nerves are in such disarray!*

I remain confined to bed-rest in my rooms. Suzette changes my dressings and brings me beef consommé with millet bread for supper.

"Did you really see him, Madame?" she asks one evening, gaze firmly fixed on the bandage she is wrapping around my palm. Several strands of straw-coloured hair have worked their way loose from her bun to lie untidily along the nape of her neck; I resist the urge to take one between my thumb and forefinger and yank. Instead I tell her that it was merely a nightmare, the product of a mind curdled with horror and grief — a mind that is fully itself once again, I hasten to add.

"You haven't seen any wraiths since?"

Though my spine itches, I do not so much as glance at the

window where Marie-Catherine has taken to standing, gaze fixed to the world outside. "No," I tell Suzette. "I have not."

Once the girl leaves, disappointed no doubt at being denied fresh gossip to dole out in the village, I turn to the creature I swore I did not see and ask her once again why, in the whole of this great and miserable house, it is my bedchamber she has chosen to frequent. I do not expect a response, or least not one that makes any kind of sense, but Marie-Catherine tilts her head and stares at me from beneath her curls. Her left eye still bulges from its shattered socket, but I no longer find myself sickened by its roll and sway; how soon atrocities become commonplace.

"Safe," she murmurs.

My palm, I notice, is already spotted afresh with red.

"She said that it's safe," I tell Henriette when she appears later that night, as she always does, to fret and fuss over her friend. "What does she mean?"

"He doesn't come into this room; she's safe from his torment in here."

"He torments her?"

Henriette favours me with a patient, sidelong stare. "Did you suppose yourself his favourite? That he waits faithful and forlorn for you to emerge from this chamber in which you have so neatly ensconced yourself?" A faint smile curves her mouth. "He torments us all. We can no more escape him in his present state than when we were alive. Not him, and not this house."

Now I know the meaning of those sounds I have too often heard of late, have too often pretended not to hear, just as my brothers pay them no obvious mind: moans and distant wails; running feet and roars of pursuit; belaboured breaths and sobs choked back in terror.

"In his present state... but has our husband not always imprisoned you?"

"He paid us no mind after our deaths; perhaps he did not even know we remained until now." Henriette frowns. "The key is cursed, and has bound all who made use of it to this house — including our husband."

"But how, when the damned thing belongs to him?"

"The butcher seldom forges his own blade." Henriette adjusts her jonquil robe, pulls the collar close about her throat so that the rope burn is all but hidden. "I cannot guess at its workings, but the key's magic does not belong to him, nor does he control it. I feel sure of that — as sure as we must now, again, bear the brunt of his ire."

Because of me, the woman does not say, because of my brothers and the doom they brought with them to this house. But had they not arrived with their sabres flashing, why then I would be as dead as Henriette and the other wives, would be lurking in the shadows the same as they once did, sharpening my tongue in anticipation of yet another wife being carried across the threshold.

And another. And another.

Though I'm loath to think of us all rubbing shoulder-to-shoulder like sardines packed in brine, I ask Henriette why the other wives do not retreat here as Marie-Catherine has done, if this room is so safe, if the thing that was our husband does not cross its threshold.

"Should we spend eternity confined to just one room? He cannot torment us all at once and turns must be taken." She surveys her surroundings and shudders. "Besides, it is... unpleasant here. This room repels at every moment."

I follow her gaze, taking in the fine and lavish furnishings I've come to know so well: the billowy blue curtains draped around my bed, its linens matched down to the last hand-stitched cornflower; the soft, padded chairs embroidered with birds and berries that surround the little table upon which I take my afternoon tea; the pale lilac drapes, now closed against the night outside. Layers of former lives, of former *wives*, meant I have never been truly at home here — or anywhere else in the house, for that matter —though since my husband's death... yes, there is something more. A constant prickle and itch, along with a vague pressure at my temples that occasionally deepens to mild nausea. Discomforting, surely, but repellent?

"It doesn't feel so terrible to me," I say. "Considering the alternative."

Henriette regards me with equanimity, one hand caressing the mark on her neck. "When you are dead, you know your place — and you know where your place is *not*."

"Marie-Catherine seems to find it agreeable."

"Perhaps only more so than the alternative." Henriette rubs her companion's back in slow and soothing circles. "Her poor mind has fractured over time; it seeps sense as a cracked vase seeps water."

"Such unkind words!"

"Such *honest* words. What use have we now for any other sort?"

From somewhere deep in the house there echoes a faint, shocked cry. Henriette straightens her shoulders and, in the span of a blink, vanishes from sight. On a rescue mission, perhaps, or else simply spurred to a more palatable hiding place, I cannot tell. I do not understand the wives and their workings any more than I understand the curse that keeps us all in this prison-house. A prickling of tears takes me by surprise, and I wipe at them savagely, pressing the heels of my hands into my eyes hard enough to spark stars.

At her place by the window, Marie-Catherine whispers a single word. "Safe."

My brothers are leaving, recalled to their garrison by orders they would ignore at their peril. Pierre, winding his pocketwatch by the parlour door, seems eager to depart, even as Charles expresses once again his reluctance to abandon me to the haunts and horrors that remain in the house. He speaks figuratively, of course. Neither of my brothers give any indication that they too can see Marie-Jeanne by the fireplace, her severed hands dripping onto the spot where my husband — our husband — was slain. The rug she stands upon has been hauled down from one of the attic rooms, worn in places and clashing with the curtains, to serve as stand-in for the new carpet ordered several days ago.

I endeavour to ignore Marie-Jeanne, thankful that she is at least keeping her tongue inside her mouth this morning.

"I have sent word to Anne," Charles is saying. "I have asked her to come."

"Why?" He has my full attention now. Not our sister, not here. "What need has she to visit?"

Again, he tells me how worried they are, he and Pierre both, how hesitant they are to leave me alone with my poor nerves so frail. My hand that remains unhealed, my refusal to leave the house even to stroll on a brotherly arm through the gardens, the troubling manner in which I have begun to stare at shadows and start at the smallest creak or sigh — all these things weigh on their minds. No, it is best that Anne come stay awhile to help me manage things.

"Our sister has a head for household affairs," Pierre adds, his voice as flat and sharp as the blade that hangs by his hip.

"But she has our mother to care for," I protest.

"Our mother can come with her. It's not as though there isn't the room."

"Just see," Charles says. "The company of other women will do you the world of good."

Behind him, Marie-Jeanne bares a red and toothsome grin.

"I've meant to ask you, Charles... that day... what made you come here?"

My brother looks uncomfortable. "I felt that we should." He moves his fingers over the nape of his neck. "There was a tickle, almost, as of someone breathing soft and close, and I felt... I felt you needed us. I cannot explain it any better."

"What does it matter?" Pierre says, clearly impatient. "You should be grateful, sister, and not question the workings of providence."

Providence, I would not think to question. The workings of wives, however, is another matter.

At the entrance door, my brothers both embrace me and, as Charles bestows a kiss upon each cheek, I look over his shoulder at the outside world, so big and bright and forbidden. A carriage with two sleek bay geldings in harness, far fancier than any our family could previously have afforded to hire, waits for them on the drive. Behind me, upstairs, someone wails.

Pierre unhooks my husband's keyring from his belt and passes to it me. "For the lady of the house." His bow is courteous but gently mocking. Anne will be here before long, that bow reminds me. Anne, with her head for household affairs.

"A key is missing," I point out.

"Your girl has it," Charles says. "There was... a stain; she was instructed to clean it."

We are not to speak of what the stain might be, his anxious face begs me, nor of which particular door the key unlocks.

I watch until the carriage disappears behind the trees that line a curve in the drive, until I can no longer hear the sound of the horses' hooves, just as I did on the morning my husband laid out his dreadful trap for me. Oh, would that I could revisit that day! That I could but take his keys, all of his keys, and leave them nestled harmless in my pocket, untried and untainted, while I sat by the fire with my needlework or played on the piano in the music room or wandered the grounds with a slim volume of poetry in hand. That I could but return them unsullied, so he might gaze at me with lustful eyes and call me his beloved and bear me up the stairs to his bed. I would put up with even that to wind back this particular clock.

If only I had kept my promise—

But no, for I remember too the gleam of bone amid rags of dark and dusty blue. The nameless wife, the first wife, who could have found nothing in that room but her own demise.

There would always have been another trap.

I summon Suzette to ask for the little brass key my brothers gave her. She tells me that it has been soaking in vinegar for a week, and it certainly smells as much when she brings it.

"It's a strange thing, Madame, these marks not coming away." The girl wipes the key on her apron one last time before handing it over. "Looks like blood — fresh blood at that — only no blood I know'll hold so quick to metal, not after a vinegar bath. I tried lye as well, and boiling in lemon juice."

"Never mind." I snatch the key from her fingers and thread it back on to its ring with the others where it gleams as bold as

Suzette's ill-hidden smile. "Find me paper, pen and ink," I tell her. "I shall be in my room."

It's laborious and frustrating, crafting the letter to Anne with only the use of my clumsy left hand. The ink smears beneath my skin until I learn to turn the page at just the right angle, and the resulting letters appear to have been scratched out by an orphan child. Still, I persevere, advising my sister that there is no need for her to endure the disruption of such a long and arduous journey, let alone to uproot our poor invalid mother. Our brothers worry for no reason. Other than my injured hand, which is admittedly slow to heal, I am in good health and have the company of a jovial and stalwart housekeeper. They should visit when our mother is feeling better, perhaps in the spring when the gardens will be in glorious bloom. In the spring, yes. I shall send for them then.

My throat tightens around a sob as I seal the letter and ring for Suzette. I hope my missive is enough. I hope the money I will also dispatch will reassure rather than alarm. I hope they both reach my sister in time.

She cannot come here. This house is not safe for women, living or otherwise.

I can feel when our husband is nearby. When he is, as Gabrielle puts it, *on the stalk*. If there is any one of us he favours most, it's Gabrielle with her wide doe-eyes and trembling lip, that mint-green gown billowing behind her as she flees through the halls. A miasma of desperation, of sad and submissive eagerness, surrounds the young woman — the youngest of us all, if only by measure of years spent breathing — and perhaps this is what lures him. A weakness, a softness at her core. Gabrielle is nothing if not pliant.

I have come to recognise the chill that precedes him, the rushing in my ears and the shiver of gooseflesh along my arms. I have come to know when to run. He is bolder now that my brothers have left, but Marie-Catherine is right: he never enters my bedchamber. Still, I cannot remain locked in that room for the remainder of my life. I try all the outer doors each morning, hoping that the curse will at last have waned and I will once more be able to step outside. It has not happened yet.

This morning, I've resolved to do something more.

The broad oak desk in my husband's study is filled with papers, ledgers and notebooks of which I can make little sense, but I search through it all regardless, hoping to find some clue to free myself from his magic. I shall move onto the library next, though I hold little hope of finding some black-spined grimoire sitting helpfully on the shelf.

"Those investments won't mature for some time yet, little dove."

Startled, I drop the ledger I am holding onto the floor. Charlotte is standing by my elbow, her mouth creased in a thin smile.

"I wish you would not do that."

"Do what?"

"Appear like that, without warning."

"'Tis my house, little dove. I shall *appear* how and where I like."

Ignoring her, I retrieve the ledger and run my finger down the columns of numbers and notations.

"Most will not be honoured in any case," Charlotte says. "Not with our husband now in his grave."

"Surely, that matters not? His estate must have a claim."

"So naive, little dove." She laughs, the gash in her throat raw and gaping. "Do you suppose a man such as he made his fortune wholly within the law? Or that all those with whom he dealt hold faith with contracts and courts? Press your claims, should you even understand them, and you might find your pretty head lopped neatly from your shoulders after all."

"Better that than starving to death in the streets!"

Charlotte snorts. Histrionics will help no one, she scolds, and besides, it is not as bad as that. There is a modest income to be derived from legal channels, and the hoard in my husband's safe will stretch a long way if we are frugal — longer, if we are canny. She guides me through the ledgers, pointing out which dealings should be surrendered as a loss and which paltry number might still be revived. Few of our husband's former associates will deign to deal with me, a naive widow so young and fresh, but some might yet be convinced. The secret, she says, is to be bold. But not, she cautions, *too* bold.

Her eyes glitter like jewels. Her face glows. Surrounded by figures and forecasts, Charlotte is a woman in her element.

"I... I thought you hated me," I say at last. "And here you are being so helpful."

She straightens, that skeletal smile back on her lips. "I do not especially like you, 'tis true. I do not especially like anyone in this house. But we *are* in this house, the six of us birds of a tarnished feather, with yours the only hands able to carry a coin or sign name to paper to ensure we keep it. I am not so foolish, nor so proud, as to deny this obvious fact. Nor do I intend to be evicted from my own home, even if I have little say in whom I share it with."

Umbrage is instinctive, a nasty rebuke landing so swift on my tongue I scarce have time to swallow it down. "You have a practical mind," I tell Charlotte instead, returning her smile with an icy offering of my own.

"An uncommon thing in a woman, my father was wont to say, with much the same acerbic tone as you would throw at me. But uncommon things are valuable, little dove, more so than empty pleasantries, simpering friendships or the broken vows of wives." She regards me for a moment longer, that narrow face veiled by something akin to sympathy, before vanishing with as little fanfare as she appeared.

I close the ledgers and stack them neatly on the desk. We are not to be friends, then, Charlotte and myself, nor enemies neither — and I find myself strangely relieved. There is a weightlessness in speaking the truth precisely as one wishes, in casting aside all mannered artifice and guile. A cruelty perhaps, if one chooses to hear it, but also a kindness.

Henriette is right.

Among the dead and the exiled, what use are any words but honest ones?

.　.　.

It's on the upstairs landing that I spy them — Gabrielle with her spine bent over the banister and our husband with one hand clutching her throat, the other plunged wrist-deep in her belly. Her mewling cries are those a stray kitten might make when caught by savage children, soft and plaintive, absent any hope of rescue, and it is these cries more than anything that propel me up the stairs with neither thought nor hesitation.

"Leave her be," I yell, brandishing the book I went to fetch from the library.

He turns, his mouth a gaping maw within that nest of frightful blue. My legs weaken, my stomach rolls, and — oh! — how I wish I'd simply scuttled on my way as I have so many times before upon hearing him at his games. But his hand drips red onto Gabrielle's green dress, and with each heave of her chest a coil of flesh, too pink, too glossy, peeks from the wound in her stomach. Bile burns at the back of my throat, hot and harsh and ashamed.

It is one thing to hear; it is quite another to witness.

"Leave her be," I say again, cursing the quaver in my voice. "Leave us all be."

Time stretches to a thin, taut line beneath my husband's regard.

Be bold, but not too bold.

I lift my chin, refusing to drop my gaze from his.

Then the moment snaps and he charges, his furious bellow filling my entire being with terror. I cry out, cringing behind the book as he launches a bloody fist right at my face — right *through* my face — a swift and wintry frost all that marks its passing.

Shocked, I touch my cheek. Already the flesh is warm again.

Leaning in close, my husband lets loose another ghastly roar. His mouth is black and hollow, his breath stinking of iron left to rust and rot, but this time I do not flinch. He is no longer a man before whom I must scrape and simper lest I be taught the lessons of his wrath, no longer a man who controls my fate, my fortune, with neatly manicured paws.

No longer a *man* at all.

"Ghoul," I whisper. "Leave me be."

Only after he vanishes do I realise what was changed about my husband, why he was so incoherent in his rage. His tongue — his tongue is wholly missing.

It is clear that none of the wives wish to be here, save Marie-Catherine of course, who stands in customary stillness by the window. Charlotte paces, hands on hips; Gabrielle mutters words of prayer beneath her breath; Marie-Jeanne pushes her tongue between her teeth at regular intervals, before sucking it noisily back in again. I try not to look at her. Henriette, whom I convinced to gather them all together in my bedchamber, casts me an anxious glance.

I clear my throat. "We share a common problem, the six of us."

"Seven," Marie-Catherine whispers.

Charlotte rolls her eyes. "For pity's sake."

"Wait, please. Listen." She raises a doubtful brow but makes no further motion to leave. It's a minor benediction on her part, this stretching of patience, and I hurriedly continue. "Our husband makes sport of us all, some more so than others." A nod for Gabrielle, who accepts it with a wan and trembling smile. "It is obscene; we should not stand for it."

"You speak as though we have a choice in the matter, little dove."

"I speak because we *do* have a choice in the matter. We can refuse."

Henriette shakes her head. "That might be true for you, with breath still in your body and flesh he cannot touch, but the rest of us are not so fortunate. We run, we hide, we go mad. Those are our choices."

"No, Henriette, you are wrong. Our husband once had the advantage, yes, but death has robbed him of that. He is no stronger now than any of you. He cannot hold his money, or his position, or any kind of authority over your necks any longer. Do you not see? He has no power but that which we allow him to take from us."

"Perhaps that is power enough," Henriette says, her voice subdued.

"He *is* still stronger," Gabrielle insists. "You, he can only frighten. Us, he can *hurt*."

"And you can hurt him."

"Preposterous!" Charlotte says. "These are but foolish guesses, and 'tis we who will bear the brunt of their falsehood. He is beyond our ability to harm or hinder."

"But one of you ripped out his tongue!" The women stare at me, shocked. I turn to Marie-Jeanne, who bares red-stained teeth in a smug and gory smile. "Was it you? Did you find such a gruesome revenge only fitting?"

"And how would she have done it?" Charlotte demands, striding forward to grasp Marie-Jeanne by the wrist. She holds up the woman's bloody stump. "With what instruments?"

"Then you, Henriette? Or Gabrielle?"

The two women shake their heads. Henriette seems to blanch at the mere suggestion, but Gabrielle frowns. "He has… wounds from time to time," she says, surveying her companions with a cautious glance. "But I would have never thought that one of you—"

"It was *not* one of us!" Charlotte snaps.

"One of us," Marie-Catherine echoes from her place by the window.

And, at that moment, there comes the faint but unmistakable creak of a floorboard from outside my bedchamber.

Three indignant strides see me to the door. As I swing it open, the girl leaning on the other side stumbles and nearly falls into the room. Grabbing Suzette by the upper arm, my fingers digging into her flesh with more ferocity than is entirely needed, I demand to know the reason for her clumsy espionage. More grist for the village gossip mill perhaps, or is it my brothers who are so keen to have her report — no matter, for whatever she believes she has heard, she is most assuredly mistaken.

Suzette glares at me. "It's not just what I *hear*, Madame." Her gaze shifts then, with slow deliberation, first to Charlotte, then to each of the other wives in succession, before sliding back to connect once more with my own.

I am stunned. "You — you can see them? For how long?"

"Been seeing wraiths since 'fore I had words to tell about them."

"Why didn't you say?"

The girl shrugs her shoulder, pointedly, and I let loose her arm. "Wasn't sure about you, was I? Wasn't gonna say nothing that would see me sent packing from here, or locked up in the madhouse, or worse."

Charlotte sniffs loudly. "This one is nothing more than a servant. She has no business here."

"And you're nothing more than a *lady* stupid enough to get her own throat slit."

"Suzette! How dare you speak that way!"

The girl sketches a curtsy so shallow her skirts barely skim the ground. "Beg pardon, Madame, but wraiths got no cause to feel superior to any living soul, no more than we got cause to humour them to think so. It's what you said: there's no position in being dead."

Charlotte's eyes are narrowed and dark. "I shall not stand for such insolence."

"Then leave. This house belongs to Madame, now. Leave it — if any of you are able."

My hand strikes, its mark blooming bright on the girl's cheek, though the blow was awkward and would scarce have hurt near as much as intended. "You are the one who shall leave," I tell her. "*I* will not tolerate such ill manners towards any person in my home, living or otherwise. Collect your belongings and depart this hour."

Suzette rubs at her face. "I can help."

"In what manner?"

She looks around the room once more, capturing the attention of each of us in turn, and when finally she replies, it's with a voice as quiet and unruffled as a millpond. "I can help you be rid of him for good."

Oh, how I wish to believe her — but what would a lowly village girl know about ghosts, let alone the unfinished business that lingers between husbands and wives? She has not used the key; for all she thinks she can see, she is not privy to everything that has happened in this house.

"I have had my fill of nonsense for one day," Charlotte says.

"Look." From her apron pocket, Suzette retrieves a golden ball no bigger than a pigeon egg and holds it up to the light.

I lean closer. "What have you there?"

"An ambuscade." She turns the thing over in her fingers. It's not a perfect sphere, its surface being marred with various dents and scratches, but there is nevertheless such an enticing, luminous quality about the little ball that I find myself reaching out a hand, wanting to hold it for myself. Quickly, Suzette tucks it back into her pocket. "It's a trap — for wraiths."

The other wives have crowded close. Even Marie-Catherine, though she has not moved from her customary position, is watching with newly focused eyes.

"Where on earth did you find such a thing?" Charlotte asks.

Henriette licks her lips. "How does it work?"

"Can we see it again?" Gabrielle pushes even closer. "Please?"

Suzette shakes her head. "I made it for him, not for you."

"*You* made it?" I am incredulous, that those same blunt fingers which each day bind my bandages fat as a winter mitten could manage such work. More like it is some bauble she has stumbled across, scooped up sly and spun a story around, though to what purpose I cannot imagine.

"If I can speak it plain, Madame, my father's a wraithwright. I learned more'n how to chop wood and slaughter chickens by watching his hands at work."

I've heard tales of such men — those who seek out haunted places, who are summoned to cleanse a stubborn, spectral stain — but assumed the most salacious details to be wholly imagined, pressed to the cause of scaring young children out of their wits, as my brothers oft delighted in doing. Of course, the once-solid floors upon which I used to so thoughtlessly tread have themselves seemed less reliable of late.

"Your father is a wraithwright."

"Yes, Madame. As was his before him."

"With the mantle now being passed on to your young shoulders, we are to suppose?"

A flicker of anger darkens her face. "He's looking for a 'prentice. Says that girls can't be what he is, that only boys got the knack for it, but that don't make sense. If only a wright can see a wraith, then aren't I one by any natural reckoning?"

"Only if I am as well, Suzette. Which I very much doubt."

"Beg pardon, Madame, but all you can see is *these* wraiths." She waves her hand around the room, mindless of the manner in which it slices right through Gabrielle's face, so close has the woman sidled in order to peek inside Suzette's apron pocket. "And that's only 'cause you're linked to them, like pearls on a string, linked to them and linked to him. It's why they're wanting my ambuscade, because of him, because it's made with—"

The girl bites off her own words, snatching her lower lip between her teeth.

"Made with what?" I grab the girl by the arm again and pull her close, then reach into her apron with my wounded hand. My fingertips flex and scrabble, shooting pain along my arm as they scoop out the ambuscade and hold it right in her face. "What did you use, Suzette?"

Around us, the wives hover and coo. *Look, dearheart, how it gleams. Can we touch it? I want to touch it.* The girl struggles to free herself, but I hold fast, demanding to know what dark magic she employed in the making of such a device — but even as I speak the words, I want to swallow them back, or I want to swallow the ambuscade, to feel it slide smooth and golden down my gullet, to know the weight of it nestled deep within my belly.

I could weep at the thought.

"Madame, here, let me take it." Her words a whisper now, gentle as a mother cat as she prises the ball from my hand. My bandage is soaked through, and she wipes the blood from the ambuscade's gilded surface before secreting it once more in her apron. "I made it from his wedding ring. His wedding ring, mixed with other scraps."

Charlotte glares at the girl. "A common thief as well, then, to steal from a dead man's hand."

"He wasn't using it no longer."

"Are we to take the words of a thief for truth? It seems an ugly bauble, and ill-made. I doubt it even works as she says."

Suzette smiles at the woman before her. "Good thing *pretty* doesn't stand for all."

"Enough," I tell the both of them.

Beside me, Henriette wets her lips. "Do you think he *could* be trapped?"

She is asking the question of me, but it's Suzette who answers. "Of course he can be trapped. Any wraith can be trapped if a person has the knowing of it. Only..." Her gaze falters for the first time since I dragged her into my bedchamber. "Only, I can't do it on my own."

She's tried to catch our husband herself, the girl explains, many times over, but he seems wholly distracted, casting about like a hound on a scent. It will take the wives and myself, the six of us — "Seven," says Marie-Catherine, largely ignored — to help corner him, to focus his attention on the ambuscade and remove all other temptation from within his grasp.

"But how do we do such a thing?" Henriette asks.

"Refuse him," Suzette says, glancing at me. "It's not really true, what Madame said before. He is still stronger than any one of you, and more powerful — he brung that through from life. But not together, not if you all stand against him at once."

Charlotte has been pacing the room with long, slow strides. Now she stops and taps a finger against her lips. "Perhaps the upstart creature seeks to ensnare us all."

Henriette shakes her head. "If that were true, she would hardly be sounding a warning."

"Do we trust her?" Gabrielle whispers. "Do we dare?"

Marie-Jeanne spits her severed tongue on to the floor and grins.

Charlotte stares at Suzette for a moment longer, brow creased with indecision, before turning to me. "I don't entirely *dis*believe the girl, but if we assist her and she fails, what fate then befalls those of us still trapped in this house with a husband whose wrath will burn even hotter?"

"I am trapped here as well, Charlotte. If he can be captured, then we might all of us be freed. At the very least, we will be free of *him*."

"We are his wives, little dove. We shall never be free of him."

With that, she is gone, followed soon after by Henriette and Gabrielle, who offers me an apologetic wave in parting. Marie-Jeanne leaves her tongue behind, and it remains for several seconds before vanishing on its own. Suzette crouches to touch a flattened palm to the empty, unmarred carpet where it lay. By the window, Marie-Catherine stares at the girl, unmoving.

"Seven," she says. "Never free."

That evening I make my way to the kitchen where I find Suzette muttering to herself as she rolls out a pie crust. The girl's sleeves are pushed up to her elbows, and I'm taken aback by the sight of those strong, bare arms working the dough. My mother used to make pies for us, before my father died and she herself became too ill, too weak for such exertions. I remember the clouds of flour that settled on the table and how Anne and I used to write our names in their soft, white leavings. My throat tightens and I clear it noisily.

By her bench, Suzette startles. "Beg pardon, Madame." She claps her palms together before wiping them on her apron. "I didn't see you."

"I've been pondering our current circumstances," I tell her. "It seems quite fortunate, provident even, that just as the need arises for a person with very *particular* expertise, why, here you are with your little trinket."

The girl picks up the rolling pin once more. "What work do you suppose there is for a wraithwright's daughter down in the village? I've only got this job 'cause no one else wanted it no more, not since the last housekeeper come back with stories of thumps and bumps and bloodcurdling screams in the night."

"Before my husband died, I myself heard nothing untoward."

"Folks like to talk big. When something isn't right with a place but they got nothing to show for it, they make it up themselves, or their imagination does. A wraithwright knows to keep an ear out, knows what stories to listen for."

"Tell me the truth."

"What truth would you be after, Madame?"

"You say you have come to trap my husband's wraith and yet you were part of this household well before I arrived, let alone before he died."

The girl folds the dough over itself before starting to roll it afresh.

"You came for the others, Suzette, did you not? For the wives?"

"I guessed there'd be a wraith here, from what folks were saying. Figured I could snare myself one to prove to Pa I could do it."

"Did you know my husband murdered them? Did you know he was planning to murder *me*?"

"No!" She seems roundly shocked at the suggestion. "They kept to themselves before he started chasing them about. I wasn't even sure who they were."

"But you suspected."

Suzette kneads the dough into a ball and pounds it onto the benchtop. "And if I did? His lordship with his title and his coin and his sly old words? Who'd have believed the likes of me over all that? Wives die all over, Madame — that's the truth you're so keen on digging out. Wives die, and the world keeps to its path."

She glares at me, cheeks flushed and fingers clenched deep in the dough, and I wonder at how a girl her age grows to be so fierce. Perhaps all children of wraithwrights are thus, born with fearsome natures to a fearsome world.

"Such an odd word when you think on it."

"Beg pardon, Madame?

"Wraithwright," I tell her. "Wraith-hunter would seem more appropriate, wraith-trapper even, if that be what such a person does. Why *wright*? What is it that's *made*?"

"Ambuscades are made. And places — they're made safe."

Her gaze flickers to the bench and back; one blink and I would have missed it.

"If you want my assistance, Suzette, or the assistance of any in this house, you would do well to speak plainly."

She gnaws on her lip. "We're not supposed to tell. It's not for ordinary folk to know."

"What is it about this situation that seems *ordinary* to you?"

"The ambuscade, it's used…" She begins to work the dough once more, her hands gentler now and careful. "It's used to make other things. Important things, valuable things."

"Such as?"

"Depends what's trapped inside. My father, he made a needle once, never laid a bad stitch. The Royal Seamstress has it, he says, but that might not be true. And, up north, I heard there was a knife made would always find a man's heart, no matter how clumsy the aim. That's rare, though, and needs a mighty powerful wraith. Most of the time it's smaller things, charms and wards — but better than you'd get with cottage magic."

"How is it done?"

"I don't know that part of it."

"Suzette…"

"I swear, Madame, on my life. I know how to craft an ambuscade fairly well but that other work…" She shrugs, but this time her gaze holds firm with mine. "That's not for anyone but wrights and 'prentices — which I'll never be 'less I bring my Pa a wraith of my own."

I cross my arms over my chest. "Then let us hope the others may yet be convinced."

"You'll talk with them, then? Persuade them?"

"Me?" Laughter comes unbidden and I cough, covering my mouth with my hand. The bandage, I notice, will need changing before dinner. "You are not a good judge of station, are you, Suzette? My words will persuade none of them, so lowly am I in their estimation. Why, I am not even dead!"

"But a wife, same as them. You still wear your wedding ring."

Frowning, I consider the slim gold band that adorns my finger. I cannot think why I have not removed it, why I have not even thought to remove it before now. It slips over my knuckle with only minor persuasion and falls onto the flour-strewn benchtop with a small puff of white. I tell Suzette to destroy it, to melt it down, or sell it and keep the coin for herself — I care not so long as I never see it again. Already, I feel lighter, closer to the girl I was before my husband ever laid his monstrous eye on me.

At the kitchen door, I turn. "One final matter, Suzette, and heed me well."

"Yes, Madame?"

"If but one of these women comes to any harm in making use of your ambuscade, you shall deeply regret ever crossing the threshold of this house. That, I promise."

"I promise, too, Madame." Her voice is solemn. "It's only *him* I want now."

Next morning, while Suzette is attending to my bandages, Charlotte appears in my bedchamber. "We are resolved to assist you," she tells me in proud, clipped tones. "This is our home, and we will no longer be chased through it like curs in need of lashing. We will no longer hide."

"You are all agreed on this?"

Charlotte glances towards Marie-Catherine, stationed by the window as usual, and sniffs. "Almost all." She makes a small movement with her chin, and Henriette materialises at her side, followed by a grinning Marie-Jeanne.

It takes Gabrielle a few moments longer and, when she does appear, her face is worried and drawn, and she has both arms hugged tightly about her waist. Blood seeps fresh over her cuffs. "What if the trap doesn't work?" she whispers. "What if—"

"It will work," Suzette says. "If we all band together, we can catch him."

Gabrielle looks doubtful. "I'm frightened."

"We're all of us frightened, dearheart." Henriette places a hand on the other woman's shoulder. "That is precisely why we must make the attempt."

"Compose yourself, Gabrielle," Charlotte says, her voice

softer and kinder than I have ever heard it. "If we succeed, you need never bear the brunt of our husband's desires again — not you nor any one of us. This place is not our home if we are forced to live in it as prey."

Gabrielle nods. "It may as well be our prison."

"And we our own bailiffs."

The exchange has a well-worn quality to it, as though these same words have been trod over for many an hour. Still, Charlotte seems satisfied as she turns to thrust a finger towards Suzette. "You, girl, bring forth that bauble of yours and teach us its workings."

I marvel at her bearing; if not for the handicap of her sex, Charlotte would have made a fine general, able to cajole and command in equal measure. With all agreed, it seems, we fall to strategy. Suzette and Charlotte jar and scrape against each other's hulls, but the girl manages to curb her temper more times than not, and the other woman allows the lack of deference she receives to pass, if not unnoticed, then mostly unremarked. At one point, Marie-Jeanne catches my eye and, with a wink, pokes her tongue out between her teeth. Gruesome as her visage is, I find myself smiling.

Over by the window, Marie-Catherine ignores us completely.

Later, after the wives have departed to prepare themselves as best they can, Suzette retrieves what appears to be a necklace from her pocket. It is a decidedly unattractive thing — a blunt and battered piece of gold strung on leather thong. "I made this for you, Madame, for you to wear."

Trying to mask my dismay, I accept it from her hand. "Suzette, I..."

"It's a talisman, to keep you safe. To keep you hidden from what would hurt you." The girl licks her lips. "I used your wedding band."

Holding it up to the light, I notice a series of symbols scratched into one side. I have no idea what they mean, or what their purpose might entail, but I take a strange kind of comfort in their shaky, ill-carved lines.

"Pretty doesn't stand for all," Suzette says in a low and hopeful voice.

I smile and pass the necklace back to her. "Please, my hand is too clumsy for knots." Sitting very still, I close my eyes as Suzette ties the thong around my throat. Her breath, so close and warm on the nape of my neck, feels like something akin to trust.

The basement chamber is no less cold than when first I stepped across its threshold, but this time at least it is clean — an improvement no doubt due to Suzette, on her hands and knees with a hard-bristled brush and bucket after bucket of tepid water hauled down the stairs, scrubbing until all blood was banished. Such a grisly chore and yet here she stands, round face so stoic in the flicker of candlelight you would suspect her to have witnessed no sight in her young life more gruesome than a sackful of drowned puppies.

Charlotte offers me a curt nod, then leads Henriette and Marie-Jeanne into the shadows on the far side of the chamber where they all but disappear. Marie-Catherine, as suspected, has refused to take part — although *refused* is perhaps too deliberate a word to describe the habitual silence she keeps — and Gabrielle is on the stalk.

If indeed a deer can ever be said to be truly stalking a wolf.

"I would see it again."

Suzette opens her fist to show me the ambuscade nestled within. "Please, Madame, stop fretting." She closes her fingers around the lumpy golden ball once more and drops her hand to her side. "It'll be made right, I swear."

"*If* Gabrielle can find him. *If* she can lure him down—"

There resounds a roar from beyond the chamber door, and then the two of them come flying in: Gabrielle with arms outstretched and mint green dress sailing in her wake, our husband barely a pace behind. His fingers tangle in her hair, wrenching her back against his chest, and she cries out in pain and shock, her eyes wide with terror. I scarce have time to note the new alteration to his visage, those scarlet slashes running so deep through his cheek that the bone glistens white within, before the others are upon him.

Screeching like Valkyries from their corner, they descend with teeth bared and fingers hooked, Charlotte leading the charge but Marie-Jeanne and Henriette fast at her heels, and Gabrielle too now turning upon her attacker. The four of them rend and pummel and tear until our husband lets loose a guttural wail and makes to retreat — to no avail, for wherever he turns there is yet another wife, the full force of her fury unleashed at last upon the man who has trapped her all these years, who has refused her the peace that death promises in preference to his own vile pleasures.

"See here," Suzette steps forward, holding the ambuscade on her outstretched palm. "See! See here!"

And see he does, those great blue eyes round as dinner plates heaped full with longing, with desire bolder than I have witnessed before. He endeavours to wrest himself free, but the wives will not relent, so enraptured are they now in their own vengeful pursuit that all our careful plans seemed tossed awry.

"Charlotte!" The name shoots from my lips almost of its own volition, it seems, and I shout it again, and again, until finally the woman turns her head to fix me with a glazed and ill-focused stare. "Charlotte," I say once more, my tone lower now, "Charlotte, please. *Stop.*"

She blinks and shakes her head. Then withdraws, placing a hand on Henriette's shoulder as she does so, pulling the other woman back with her, and their husband, my husband, *our husband no more*, takes his opportunity and—

—is gone.

In Suzette's hand, the ambuscade gleams brighter than the candle flame.

"Is he... ?"

The girl nods. "He's trapped. It's done." She looks up, grinning wide, and an immense wave of relief shudders through me. Until — oh! — her face contorts, mouth set in a grimace as though someone has caught each side in fish-hooks and is pulling downward, pulling her whole body down to the flagstones where she begins to flail and fit. Crouching at her side, I grasp the girl by the shoulders and try to still her thrashing while the wives hover about us like all-too-anxious aunts.

"What is happening to her? Why does she writhe like that?"

"Is this his doing?"

"But he is trapped — see how the ambuscade glows."

"Perhaps he is stronger than she thought."

"And furious, oh! How furious he will be with us!"

As suddenly as she began, Suzette stops her shaking and stares at me, a thin line of saliva suspended from her lower lip. Her eyes are raw, their whites shot through with blood, their pupils huge and black.

"Suzette, what is the matter?"

I flinch as she raises her fist, and the ambuscade is in her mouth before I realise her purpose — but realise it I do or, more truly, recognise it: that queer desire to subsume the thing into myself, and so my own fingers follow it, doing battle with tongue and teeth until at last I grasp the thing, all slippery and slick, and wrench it from her. As the girl moans and falls back, her sudden fire extinguished, there comes a curious, fleeting pressure against my sternum, like the muzzle of a disappointed hound, snuffling and searching and moving swiftly on. Beneath the bodice of my gown, the talisman grows warm.

Suzette drags herself several paces, chest heaving, then vomits into the corner. The smell of urine wafts from her skirts.

"What was that?" I ask her. "What did he do to you?"

The girl swallows, wipes at her mouth. "Not him," she croaks at last. "That was *her.*"

Behind us, the chamber door slams shut with a sharp, resounding crack that I feel to the marrow of my bones.

First Wife. Whose name is lost, whose family is unknown. Whose honour will remain besmirched.

"But *where* is she?" Charlotte asks. "None of us have ever so much as sensed her presence in this house."

"She's everywhere." Suzette frowns, rubs her lips together. "She... she *is* this house. She's soaked into every tile and floorboard, every nail and window pane; you can't sense her no more than a fish knows the water it swims in." The girl looks at me. "But, Madame, I reckon your bedchamber's her very heart. I reckon that's why the others don't like it there, why your husband's wraith couldn't pass its threshold."

"Marie-Catherine likes it there," Gabrielle retorts.

Henriette shakes her head. "I do not think she likes it; I think she endures it."

"Can you make an ambuscade for her — for First Wife?" I ask.

"She's not a wraith," Suzette says. "She's not any kind of thing I know how to snare."

There comes another loud crash from upstairs, the third or fourth since the door was locked against us, and I jump as I have each time before. All of it is First Wife's doing, according to Suzette: the blood on the key, which now refuses to turn in the lock, and how all of us have been kept prisoner in this house; no one who dies here gets to leave, nor does any living wife once she sates her curiosity with a peek into the one place her husband forbade her. For if it was to be *her* fate, this matrimonial murder most foul, most unfair, then why should any other suffer less? No one shall leave, not any of us and certainly not her husband. Too many years have been spent in patient anticipation, waiting for the right time, for the right wife to bring with her the necessary tools for her husband's demise.

She wishes to take her time tearing him to pieces.

"She's nothing but pain and rage and hate," the girl says. "You hurt a person bad enough, they stop being a person at all. Vengeance is all she is now."

"And we have robbed her of even that." I squeeze the ambuscade in my good fist. Suzette has left the tiny globe in my keeping; the talisman I wear seems to veil it well enough — from both First Wife and my own urges. "She waited all this time and we took him from her."

"You cannot know any of this," Charlotte says. "'Tis nothing more than idle speculation."

Suzette glares at the woman. "You try having her inside o'

you, squirming 'bout like a belly full o' polecats all fixing to sink their fangs. I know what she is now, and what she wants. I know it more'n anyone here and I won't be having it said elsewise."

"It's worse than it ever was," Gabrielle wails. "We had the whole house to hide from him, and now we're trapped in this awful room where... where..." As she begins to sob, Marie-Jeanne drifts to her side. She presses her cheek against the other woman's shoulder and hums, a soft and comforting tune that I remember my mother singing to me as a child. Gabrielle clutches Marie-Jeanne's arm and sobs harder.

She is right. This is worse. We cannot stay here, two living women and four dead ones — eventually to be six dead if we cannot figure an exit from this chamber that stinks of vomit and urine and fear. Wrestling with Suzette has caused the wound in my right hand to bleed most generously, and my mouth is dry with thirst.

"We have to reason with her," I say. "It makes no sense to punish us along with him; we are his victims as much as she was."

"You can't reason with what she is, Madame."

"Then perhaps we can bargain." I march across to the marble basin, scrubbed as clean now as the rest of the room.

"Madame, no!"

Ignoring the girl, I place the ambuscade in the empty bowl where it rolls a little before coming to rest in the centre. "First Wife," I whisper. The stale air presses close about me, and I clear my throat. "First Wife, see what I have here." The room chills, the skins on my arms itches.

She is listening.

"You may have him," I tell her. "You may have him all to yourself. But first you must deliver us our liberty." I glance behind me: the wives, clustered together, are watching. "All of us, those with breath and those without. For we are as you find yourself — most grievously wronged."

The air tears apart with a shriek as the basin is lifted two clear feet above the floor then thrown against the wall with such force that the marble shatters, sending pieces ricocheting across the room. I touch a hand to my cheek; it comes away red. Gabrielle is weeping again, and Suzette is crawling through the rubble, fingers frantically searching, until — there! — a faint glow, and I hasten to her side, crouching to take hold of her wrist. "Do not touch it! Remember the last time." Instead, I retrieve the thing myself, dust it clean on my skirts.

"First Wife." My voice is stronger now. "Release us from this place, from this house, and we shall surrender our husband to your keeping. You cannot retrieve him yourself now; you must realise that. If you keep us locked in this chamber until we are all of us wraiths, what will that gain you?"

Nothing, for near too long. Gabrielle begins to speak but Suzette shushes her. My temples throb.

"You have my word," I say. The bandage on my injured hand is half undone. Wincing, I unwrap it the rest of the way, cross my wounded palm to my breast. "My blood oath, as one wife to another. He was your husband first; he will be yours to the last."

The pressure in my head eases, the chill lifts from the room.

And the great chamber door creaks open.

The house is in utter disarray. Drapery has been torn from the windows and furniture flung about as though by a giant's fist, while the dining room chandelier glitters in shards on the table, and half the balustrade lies in splinters over the stairs. Suzette and I pick our way with care. Charlotte and the other wives glide easily in our wake.

"Why destroy the house now?" I mutter. "She hasn't so much as blown a candle out before."

"She *is* the house, Madame. Would you pull out your own hair? Your own fingernails? She must be desperate to be tearing herself apart."

"Desperate?" Charlotte snorts. "Spiteful, perhaps."

"Spite's got nothing to do with it," Suzette says. "It's fury and frustration that makes her mad."

"But if she can do all this..." I wave at the destruction around us. "Why did she not dispense with our husband years ago? He was a man; murderous and evil, but still a man. His neck would have broken clean as any other's."

Suzette rubs at her forehead. "I don't think she could. It felt like... like his death made her this way, made her stronger. Made her... *full*." Her voice lowers to a whisper. "Let's leave, Madame. Break a window if that's what's needed, but please... let's leave now."

Charlotte clears her throat. "Is it *she* or merely us that you suppose hard of hearing?"

"Enough," I say. "Suzette, let us be done with this." Though clearly miserable, the girl nods. I touch her shoulder. "It's the only way. She will allow none of us to leave otherwise, which will likely be the least of our troubles."

The bedchamber is so cold my breath frosts the air. The ceiling-high window where Marie-Catherine stands watch is shattered, its curtains torn on the jagged splinters caught in the wooden frame. Their tattered shreds flap and tussle in the winter breeze, and yet she does not move from their path, does nothing but turn her head as our motley brigade enters the room, her gaze shifting through us and past us just as surely as the curtains slice through her spectral form. Henriette rushes to her side, clasps one of Marie-Catherine's hands within her own, but whatever words she finds to whisper into her friend's ear remain unacknowledged.

Gently, I push Suzette forward. For the first time, there is more than just discomfort in this chamber; I can sense the profound unease of which the wives have spoken. The skin on the back of my neck prickles, and I recall the last time I saw Charles and the way his fingers scratched at the air over his own nape, and wonder if the phantom breath of which he spoke felt equally chill. Was it really true that none of my predecessors had brothers or fathers nearby at their moment of need — or, rather, at *hers*? I do not wish to think upon the number of wives who might have followed had I, too, been bereft of kin to summon to her vengeful cause. The poker my husband wielded had such a sharp hook; I would not have made a pretty wraith.

Sitting cross-legged on the floor, Suzette smooths her skirts neatly about herself before holding out her hand. With only the barest hesitation, I lean over and place the ambuscade upon her palm.

Whatever dread event I was expecting, it does not manifest. The room remains cold. The wind continues to blow through the broken window. The wives keep watch in silence.

Letting loose a long, tremulous breath, Suzette closes her eyes and rolls the ambuscade between her hands as though it is a tiny ball of dough. All the while she mutters, words that rumble low and deep, their meaning well beyond my comprehension, and after a time the sphere seems to elongate between her palms, its shape stretching well beyond true. It glows brighter than before, brighter than the first peek of dawn, and the warmth it radiates draws me closer, closer, until I am crouching right beside the girl, fixed to the working of her hands. Their motions are wondrous strange.

When first it appears, the crack is thinner than an eyelash and scarce as long, and as I watch a fine tendril of mist snakes forth, describing a lazy spiral towards the ceiling.

"Suzette, look..."

The girl's eyes widen, as though she did not truly anticipate the success of her ministrations. Then she shakes her head, tears welling. "No," she whispers. "I won't let it go. I thought I could, but... I need him." And her hands close tight.

"You must continue. We have given our word."

"Your word, not mine." The girl drops her gaze. "I'm not a wife; I didn't use the key. *I* could leave."

Even as I reach for her, desperately trying to prise her fingers apart with my own — because she cannot leave, she *cannot* — Suzette lets forth an awful moan and starts to shake, her body rocking violently back and forth. First Wife, wronged and wrathful — surely, this time she will not release the girl.

"Suzette," I shout, inches from her face. "Let him loose. Let him loose now!"

The talisman sways between us, and I wrench it over my head, cheeks chafed by the leather thong, in the hope that it will shield Suzette from First Wife as well as it does me. But there is no time to give it to her: the moment the necklace leaves my person, that wrathful focus narrows and pivots and then—

—I'm flying across the room, slamming against the wall with such force I fear I may never breathe again.

The talisman falls from my hand.

One of the wives screams.

Suzette is shrieking as well, and I wrap my arms around my head, trying to blot it out, trying to blot everything out, the noise and the sharp new pain that pierces my side with each hard-drawn gasp, until—

—silence. Or nearly so, just a faint, delicate keening.

Marie-Catherine kneels before Suzette, who is swaying only slightly now with lips parted slack around the reedy noise she makes. "Stop," the woman murmurs as she stares into the girl's terrified eyes, into the eyes of the being that hides within. "Stop now. It is done. It is done."

Suzette's hands fall open.

The ambuscade tumbles, bounces, and—

splits

—and here he comes, my husband, our husband, *her* husband, coalescing in mid-air with the tormented roar of a lion caged. Wheeling around, he takes all of us in, his wives, and that vicious snarl narrows to a sneer. I force myself to my feet, determined to stand between whatever evil he intends and the women upon whom he would visit it. But no need — oh! — no need, for that same force which tossed me as readily as an autumn leaf now ensnares him in its grip and tears him quite asunder.

Blood falls, red and dry as spectral rain. The whole house shudders and shakes. And falls into satisfied silence.

I stumble over to where Suzette lies, curled tight and whimpering. "Hush, come now." Teeth clenched against the stabbing pain in my side, I pull the girl to her feet. "We must leave."

She coughs. "There's no rush, madame. She has what she wants."

"My husband? Did you not see? She has done away with him simple as blinking — she will vent her wrath on us next."

"No, she merely plays — a cat with a mouse. As she has done before."

I consider his missing tongue, and the deep scratches in his cheeks. Charlotte steps forward. "You cannot kill what is already dead, little dove."

"And if she seeks other mice with which to play?"

"This is my home. I intend to remain here."

"And you, Marie-Catherine?"

The woman in the pale peach dress smiles and pushes her hair away from her face. Her mutilated eye is no easier to witness. "We are safe. We are *all* safe." The ghost of a smile flashes across her mouth. "All but *him*."

"Madame!" Suzette grabs my right wrist, her face alight with wonder. "See!"

And I do. For the first time since my husband pressed his burning key into my palm — *her* key, *her* tireless wounded magic all this time — the sore has ceased its constant bleeding. A clear fluid still weeps from its centre, but the edges are miraculously crusted and dry.

My hand, at long last — my poor little hand is healing.

It should come as less of a surprise to me that the remains of my husband's wealth smooths many paths. It kept him in wives for years, after all, kept both the curious and the priggish from his door in equal measure. And of course it paved the neat and slippery road upon which I found my own self, skating with girlish naivety into his arms on the promise of a life easier led — a most cardinal sin, judging by the sanctimonious looks Suzette and I receive upon stumbling into the village, to wish for safety, for security, to value such things above the luxurious romance of love.

But for the midwife who stitched the cut in my cheek and fussed over my fractured ribs, who provided a basin of warm water for the both of us to bathe the grime from our bodies, a coin pressed into her palm means a new roof for her cottage and several young chickens to provide her with eggs each morning.

For the constabulary to whom I reported the ransacking of my house by brigands unknown, and who undertook with oaths solemnly sworn to keep regular watch over the premises in my most understandable absence, a handful of gold will procure two swift steeds for the stables.

For the men engaged to repair the windows and board up the premises, as well as for the broad-shouldered warden who will stalk the grounds with his dogs of a night, my husband's money makes plentiful the food on their dinner tables and well-made the clothes on the backs of their families.

I was never alone in my desire for security.

Across from me in our newly acquired carriage, Suzette slumps and snores. The girl is exhausted and I do not begrudge her the rest I cannot yet find for myself, so tumultuous are my thoughts. Two letters awaited me in the village for several days, both from my sister, Anne. The first advised that our mother's illness had worsened considerably and, though it pained her to defy the urgent summons of our dear brother, neither she nor our mother would be able to visit. If it were at all possible, might I come to them for a few days instead? The second, scrawled in obvious haste, expressed relief that I no longer had need of her immediate presence and thanked me for the sum I had sent — she suspected it might be put to use in part in the arrangement of our mother's funeral, so dire is her condition. She failed to understand why I had not sent word, why I had not come.

I hope our mother is still alive; I hope the four horses pulling us through the night are fast enough.

If not, I hope Anne will forgive me.

"You should sleep, dearheart," Henriette says. She has sat beside me for the entire distance, gaze fixed to the rushing world beyond the window. Even now, when there are only stars and the shadows of branches to see, she does not look away. Gabrielle and Marie-Jeanne flit in and out of the carriage as suits their whims, perching at times upon the roof or squeezing in beside our oblivious coachman. My talisman, fashioned from the wedding band our husband gave and took from each of us in turn, is enough to provide them an anchor — though for how long

Suzette cannot say. *Wraiths without a place get windblown, Madame. Only the dead know what happens after that.* Even so, none of the three wished to remain behind in the house where they had been so gruesomely murdered. Perhaps they will like the home I will share once again with my mother and sister. Perhaps they will find an anchor there.

"I see too many things when I close my eyes," I say to Henriette.

"They will diminish in time," she replies. "I can assure you of that."

I trace a finger over the key-shaped scar in my palm and think of First Wife, stalking her husband for eternity, tearing him to vengeful shreds over and over again and, with him, what remains of herself. I think of Charlotte and Marie-Catherine, and hope they are safe. I have promised to keep the house for them, and for First Wife, as long as I am able.

Some things will never diminish. Some wounds will never heal.

I close my eyes regardless and wait for sleep. If the wind does not blow too harshly, I might yet find for myself a place in this world.

ABOUT THE AUTHOR

Kirstyn McDermott has been working in the darker alleyways of speculative fiction for much of her career. She is the author of two award-winning novels, *Madigan Mine* and *Perfections*, and a collection of short fiction, *Caution: Contains Small Parts*. Her stories and poetry have been published in various magazines, journals and anthologies both within Australia and internationally, with her most recent work being *Never Afters*, a series of novellas that retell classic

Photo by Paul Ewins

fairy tales. She holds a PhD in creative writing with a research focus on re-visioned fairy tales and produces and co-hosts a literary discussion podcast, The Writer and the Critic. Kirstyn lives in Ballarat, Australia, with fellow writer Jason Nahrumg and two distinctly non-literary felines. She can be found online at www.kirstynmcdermott.com.

ALSO BY KIRSTYN MCDERMOTT

Perfections

Madigan Mine

Caution: Contains Small Parts

Triquetra

THANK YOU FOR BUYING THIS BRAIN JAR PRESS CHAPBOOK

To receive special offers, bonus content, and info on
new releases and other great reads, visit us
online at www.BrainJarPress.com

9 781922 479310